1/27

My Own Book of Animal Stories

My Own Book of Animal Stories

Edited by Lesley O'Mara

BACK
PACK
BOOKS

For Lucie

The Editor wishes to thank Michael Glover, Anne Forsyth and E. A. Prost, who helped to make this selection.

First Published in 1991 by
Michael O'Mara Books Limited, 9 Lion Yard,
Tremadoc Road, London SW4 7NQ

My Own Book of Animals Stories © 1991 Michael O'Mara Books Limited

This edition published in 2004 by Backpack Books by arrangement with Michael O'Mara Books

Cover design by Zoe Quayle
Typeset by Florencetype, Devon
Design by Mick Keates

Backpack Books
122 Fifth Avenue
New York, NY 10011

ISBN 1-5661-9572-1

Printed and bound in Singapore by Tien Wah Press

04 05 06 07 08   10 9 8 7 6 5 4 3 2 1

CONTENTS

Elephant Big and Elephant Little   Anita Hewett   6

The Lion and his Friends   Anne Forsyth   19

Pig says Positive   Anita Hewett   26

The Ossopit Tree   Stephen Corrin   34

Monkeying About   Stephen Corrin   41

The Three Little Pigs   Traditional   46

The Clever Fox   Traditional   58

The Hare and the Tortoise   Traditional   63

How the Polar Bear Became   Ted Hughes   70

The Shooting   Roald Dahl   80

Dragons and Giants   Arnold Lobel   94

The Friendliest Dog in the World   Anne Forsyth   102

Tim Rabbit's Party   Alison Uttley   112

The Proud and Fearless Lion   Ann and Reg Cartwright   126

Robert's Winter Coat   Michael Glover   140

Henny-Penny   Traditional   152

Millions of Cats   Wanda Ga'g   161

Acknowledgments   176

Illustration Acknowledgments   176

ELEPHANT BIG AND ELEPHANT LITTLE

Anita Hewett

Elephant Big was always boasting.

"I'm bigger and better than you," he told Elephant Little.
"I can run faster, and shoot water higher out of my trunk, and
eat more, and . . ."

"No. You can't!" said Elephant Little.

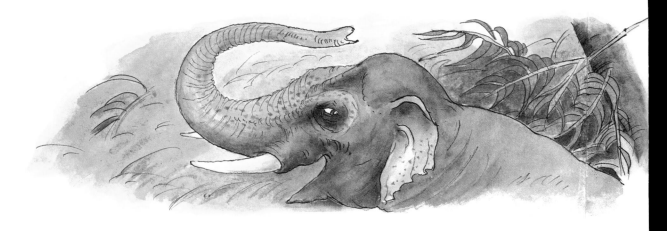

Elephant Big was surprised. Elephant Big was *always* right. Then he curled up his trunk and laughed and laughed.

"What's more, I'll show you," said Elephant Little. "Let's have a running race, and a shooting-water-out-of-our-trunks race, and an eating race. We'll soon see who wins."

"I shall, of course," boasted Elephant Big. "Lion shall be judge."

"The running race first!" Lion said. "Run two miles there and two miles back. One of you runs in the field, the other one runs in the forest. Elephant Big shall choose."

Elephant Big thought and thought, and Elephant Little pretended to talk to himself: "I hope he chooses to run in the field, because *I* want to run in the forest."

When Elephant Big heard this, he thought: "If Elephant Little wants very much to run in the forest, that means the forest is best." Aloud he said: "I choose the forest."

"Very well," said Lion. "One, two, three. Go!"

Elephant Little had short legs, but they ran very fast on the springy smooth grass of the field.

Elephant Big had long, strong legs, but they could not carry him quickly along through the forest. Broken branches lay in his way; thorns tore at him; tangled grass caught at his feet. By the time he stumbled, tired and panting, back to the winning post, Elephant Little had run his four miles, and was standing talking to Lion.

"What ages you've been!" said Elephant Little. "We thought you were lost."

"Elephant Little wins," said Lion.

Elephant Little smiled to himself.

"But I'll win the next race," said Elephant Big. "I can shoot water much higher than you can."

"All right!" said Lion. "One of you fills his trunk from the river, the other fills his trunk from the lake. Elephant Big shall choose."

Elephant Big thought and thought, and Elephant Little pretended to talk to himself: "I hope he chooses the river, because *I* want to fill my trunk from the lake."

When Elephant Big heard this, he thought: "If Elephant Little wants very much to fill his trunk from the lake, that means the lake is best."

Aloud he said: "I choose the lake."

"Very well!" said Lion. "One, two, three. Go!"

Elephant Little ran to the river and filled his trunk with clear, sparkling water. His trunk was small, but he spouted the water as high as a tree.

Elephant Big ran to the lake, and filled his long, strong trunk with water. But the lake water was heavy with mud, and full of slippery, tickly fishes. When Elephant Big spouted it out, it rose only as high as a middle-sized thorn bush. He lifted his trunk and tried harder than ever. A cold little fish slipped down his throat, and Elephant Big spluttered and choked.

"Elephant Little wins," said Lion.

Elephant Little smiled to himself.

When Elephant Big stopped coughing he said: "But I'll win the next race, see if I don't. I can eat much more than you can."

"Very well!" said Lion. "Eat where you like and how you like."

Elephant Big thought and thought, and Elephant Little pretended to talk to himself: "I must eat and eat as fast as I can, and I mustn't stop; not for a minute."

Elephant Big thought to himself: "Then I must do exactly the same. I must eat and eat as fast as I can, and I mustn't stop; not for a minute."

"Are you ready?" asked Lion. "One, two, three. Go!"

Elephant Big bit and swallowed, and bit and swallowed, as fast as he could, without stopping. Before very long, he began to feel full up inside.

Elephant Little bit and swallowed, and bit and swallowed. Then he stopped eating and ran round a thorn bush three times. He felt perfectly well inside.

Elephant Big went on biting and swallowing, biting and swallowing, without stopping. He began to feel very, very funny inside.

Elephant Little bit and swallowed, and bit and swallowed. Then again he stopped eating, and ran round a thorn bush six times. He felt perfectly well inside.

Elephant Big bit and swallowed, and bit and swallowed, as fast as he could, without stopping once, until he felt so dreadfully ill inside that he had to sit down.

Elephant Little had just finished running around a thorn bush nine times, and he still felt perfectly well inside. When he saw Elephant Big on the ground, holding his tummy and groaning horribly, Elephant Little smiled to himself.

"Oh, I do like eating, don't you?" he said. "I've only just started. I could eat and eat and eat and eat."

"Oh, oh, oh!" groaned Elephant Big.

"Why, what's the matter?" asked Elephant Little. "You look queer. Sort of green! When are you going to start eating again?"

"Not a single leaf more!" groaned Elephant Big. "Not a blade of grass, not a twig can I eat!"

"Elephant Little wins," said Lion.

Elephant Big felt too ill to speak.

17

After that day, if Elephant Big began to boast, Elephant Little smiled, and said: "Shall we have a running race? Shall we spout water? Or shall we just eat and eat and eat?"

Then Elephant Big would remember. Before very long, he was one of the nicest, most friendly elephants ever to take a mud bath.

THE LION AND HIS FRIENDS

Anne Forsyth

Once upon a time, there was a lion who lived in a great house with one little cat. "I am the King of Beasts," he said. "It is only right that I should have a grand house. And I am tired of living in the wild."

The little cat was supposed to be his servant, but he didn't do any work at all. He just lay on the best sofa and slept all day.

One day, the lion said to himself, "I am often lonely. Why should I live in a great house with only one little cat for company? Why should other animals have to live in the deep, dark jungle? Why should pigs live in the sty, and monkeys in trees and rabbits in burrows? We should all live together, and be friendly and help one another."

So he said to the little cat, "I have an idea. I am going to send out a message and ask all the other animals to come and stay. I'll ask the birds too. We will live together in peace, and be friends."

The little cat yawned. He did not think this was a very good idea, but he didn't say anything.

So the lion sent out a command, and because he was King of Beasts, the animals and birds obeyed.

The leopard came, carrying on his back the rabbit and bird and one of the monkeys. "This is not a good idea," said the leopard gloomily. "It will end in trouble."

"This is not a good idea," said the hedgehogs, who usually went to sleep in winter, but woke up when they heard of the lion's command.

"This is not a good idea," said the wise old owl. "But," he said, "the King of Beasts has called us and we must go. Too-whit too-whooo!"

The lion had been busy getting ready for the arrival of the animals. He would never be lonely again.

The zebras arrived first. "We are usually last," said the father zebra, "because 'zebra' begins with a 'z'. We are last in the alphabet, last in the picture books."

"But this time you are first," said the lion. "Come in."

The giraffe found it was impossible to get into the house, no matter how he bent his long neck. "Oh dear," said the lion, "I didn't think of that. Never mind – there is plenty of room in the barn, and a very high roof."

The giraffe sniffed. He hadn't come all this way to sleep in the barn, but the lion was the King of Beasts, so he didn't say anything, just sulked.

21

Everyone crowded into the big dining room for supper. There was fish, which pleased the penguins, and nuts and vegetables for those who didn't like fish. Some animals ate too much – the pig gobbled the monkeys' share and they chattered angrily until the lion said, "Now, now, there's plenty of food for everyone," and went back to the kitchen for more.

Afterwards they all fell asleep, some on the sofas, some on the chairs and some on the beds. But there wasn't room for everyone, and the tigers got cross because they didn't like being next to the hippos who snored loudly.

The lion found that there wasn't room for him because the leopards had taken over his room. But he didn't say anything. "They are my friends," he said to himself. "Why shouldn't they have the best beds?" And he went out and slept in the barn among the straw.

Inside, on the very best sofa, slept the little cat and his friends whom he had invited into the grand house.

It was nearly Christmas, and the lion was determined that it would be the very best Christmas ever. There would be turkey and plum pudding and decorations and paper hats and lots of games, and of course stockings for everyone.

He tried to get his friends to help. "Would you like to go and gather holly?" he asked the monkeys. "No, thank you," they said, swinging lazily from the chandeliers.

"Perhaps you would like to stir the pudding," said the lion, a little timidly, to the pandas. "No, thank you," they said, quite politely, and went back to chewing up the bamboo shoots in the garden.

So the lion decided that he would have to do everything

himself. He bought the food and made the cake and the pudding and stuffed the turkey and filled the stockings. It was very hard work. It was no joke finding a stocking for a giraffe and enough gifts to fill it.

By Christmas Day there seemed to be animals everywhere – in the house, in the kitchen, in the stables. The parrots chattered all the time, and so did the monkeys. The other animals complained of the noise. "Now, now, we must all be friends," said the lion, who was getting a little tired of it himself.

The wise old owl forgot to be wise and patient and got very bad-tempered. "There are too many birds and too many animals," he said.

By Christmas night the lion was quite worn out. It was very tiring having so many friends to stay.

Next day the tiger cubs and the leopard cubs fell out over their Christmas toys: the little mother monkey spoke sharply to the pig about his table manners. The zebra's feelings were hurt because of something the antelope had said: and the giraffe was sulking again.

"This won't do," said the tiger. He was next in line to the King of Beasts and thought himself just as good as the lion any day. So he hired a boat and said, "I'm off – anyone else want to come?"

They all crammed into the boat, the monkeys swinging from the rigging. And then they set sail, leaving the lion in his great house. The boat called at a number of ports, so that the farm animals could go back to the farm, the jungle animals to the jungle and the woodland creatures back to the woods.

Back at the house, the lion looked around him. Everything was upside down. The animals had smashed the best crockery. The very best chair had been broken when the elephant sat on it. The carpets had been trodden by the hooves of all the zebras and ponies.

He sighed. "Lions should live in the open, not in houses," he said to himself, and he crept out of the grand house, back to the wild, leaving everything behind him. He swished his tail as he went and sang a little song to himself. He felt more cheerful already. It was good to be free again.

Behind him, in the grand house, the little cat went back to sleep.

PIG SAYS POSITIVE   Anita Hewett

Monkey sat in a coconut tree. Below, on the ground, sat
Peccary Pig.

"Pig, will it rain today?" asked Monkey. "I want to go to
the jungle clearing, to plant a coconut under the ground. But
I can't plant my coconut today unless there is rain to make
it grow."

"Rain?" said Peccary Pig. "It might."

Monkey picked a coconut, and ran through the jungle with
it, singing:

> "Pig says might, pig says might,
> Shut the door and bolt it tight."

26

When Monkey came to the grassland, he met a creature with short black legs, a black bushy tail, and a fat brown body.

"Hello, Sausage," Monkey called.

The creature said: "I'm Bush Dog, not Sausage. Where are you taking that coconut?"

"I'm going to plant it," Monkey told him.

"What a waste of good food; let's eat it," said Bush Dog.

Monkey looked up into the sky. There was only one small ragged raincloud.

"Very well," he agreed. "We'll share it."

"First we must roast it," Bush Dog said. "Go away and find some firewood, and I will guard the coconut."

Monkey put the coconut down, and went away to find the firewood. When he came back, Bush Dog was smiling, and Bush Dog was full of coconut. Lying behind him were two empty shells.

"You have eaten my coconut," Monkey shouted.

He threw the empty shells at Bush Dog.

"Sausage!" he shouted. And he ran through the jungle, back to his tree.

"Pig, do you *know* it will rain?" he asked.

"Know?" said Peccary Pig. "Yes, I know. I can smell it in the air. That's proof."

Monkey picked another coconut, and ran through the jungle with it, singing:

"Pig says proof, pig says proof,
Shut the door and mend the roof."

When Monkey came to the swampy land, he met a creature without a tail. His back legs were short and his front legs were long. He had shaggy brown fur and sharp curving teeth.

"Hello, Fatty," Monkey called.

"I'm Capybara," the creature said. "Where are you taking that coconut?"

"I'm going to plant it," Monkey told him.

"I think that's silly," said Capybara. "Coconuts are good to eat."

Monkey looked up into the sky. There were two black rainclouds. "We'll share it," he said.

Capybara looked at the coconut. Then he looked at Monkey's paws.

"You must wash your paws before dinner," he said. "They are muddy. Go to the lake and wash them. I will guard the coconut."

Monkey went to wash his paws. When he came back, Capybara was smiling, and Capybara was rubbing his tummy. In the mud beside him lay two empty shells.

"*Your* paws were muddy too," shouted Monkey.

He threw the shells at Capybara.

"Fatty!" he shouted. And he ran through the jungle back to his tree.

"Pig, will it rain quite soon?" he asked.

"Soon?" said Peccary Pig. "Yes, I'm certain."

Monkey picked a third coconut, and ran through the jungle with it, singing:

> "Pig says certain, pig says certain,
> Shut the door and draw the curtain."

When Monkey reached the river shell bank, he met a creature with smooth grey fur, a long bushy tail with rings around it, and paws that were very large and flat.

"Hello, Flattypaws," said Monkey.

"I'm Crab-eater Racoon," the creature said. "Where are you taking that coconut?"

"I'm going to plant it," Monkey told him.

"Plant it?" said Racoon. "How foolish! Let's eat it."

Monkey looked at the thick black rainclouds, but one little patch of sky was blue.

"Yes, we'll share it. Half each!" he said. "I shall *not* go away to gather firewood. I shall *not* go away to wash my paws. I shall stay where I am, on this shell bank."

"Of course you will," said Crab-eater Racoon. "We must split the coconut in half."

Racoon lifted his large flat paw and patted the coconut, pat-pat-pat.

"Why are you patting?" Monkey asked.

"I want to break the shell," said Racoon. "I often eat crabs, and *they* have shells. I pat-pat-pat, and pat-pat-pat, until the crab feels dreadfully tired. Then I can easily break its shell."

"Silly Racoon!" Monkey laughed. "You can't make a coconut feel tired."

"In that case," said Racoon, "it's no use to pat. You must climb to the top of a tall tree, and drop the coconut on to a stone."

"I shall *not* go away to a tree," said Monkey. "I shall stay where I am, on this shell bank."

"Just as you please," said Crab-eater Racoon. He took the coconut, went to a tree, climbed to the top, and sat on a branch.

Monkey sat on the shell bank, and waited.

He waited for quite a long time on that shell bank.

At last he called: "Hurry up, Racoon. Drop the coconut on to the stone."

Out of the tree fell two empty shells. When Monkey looked
up into the tree, Racoon was smiling, and Racoon was full.

"Greedy old Flattypaws!" Monkey shouted. And he ran
through the jungle, back to his tree.

"Pig, are you sure it will rain?" he asked.

"Sure?" said Peccary Pig. "I'm positive."

Monkey picked a fourth coconut, and ran through the jungle
with it, singing:

> "Pig says positive, pig says positive,
> Shut the door and . . ."

Monkey stopped. He could not think of a rhyme. He ran
on through the jungle, singing:

> "Pig says positive, pig says positive,
> Pig says positive, hositive, fositive . . ."

He looked around for someone to help him. But the
creatures knew that the rain was coming. They had gone to
their homes.

Monkey reached the jungle clearing. The sky was quite
covered by big black rainclouds, but Monkey did not notice
them. He did not plant his coconut. The only thing that
mattered to Monkey was finding a rhyme. So he tried again:

32

"Pig says positive, pig says positive,
Pig says positive, lositive, wositive . . ."

Drops of rain fell on his head. Plop!

"Goodness, I'm getting wet," said Monkey.

Back across the jungle he ran, home to his tree. Below the tree, Peccary Pig still sat on the ground.

Monkey climbed to a branch where the rain could not reach him. He split the coconut in half, and ate the sweet white middle of it. Only the two empty shells were left.

He threw one down, and it bounced off Pig's head and fell in the grass.

"It's a hat," called Monkey. "I knew it would rain, so I made two hats. And that one is yours."

Pig and Monkey put on their hats. Pig hummed the tune as Monkey sang:

"Pig says positive, pig has a hat,
There's the rhyme, so that is that."

Monkey felt happy. He smiled at Pig. Pig smiled back, and hummed the tune.

THE OSSOPIT TREE   Stephen Corrin

One terribly hot summer in the forests of Africa there was
a great shortage of anything to eat. The animals had been
hunting around here, there and everywhere and had finally
eaten up the very last twig and root. They were very
hungry indeed.

Suddenly they came upon a wonderful-looking tree, hung
with the most tempting, juicy-looking fruit. But, of course,

34

they didn't know whether the fruit was safe to eat or not because they had no idea what its name was. And they simply had to know its name. Luckily they did know that the tree belonged to an old lady called Jemma. So they decided to send the hare, their fastest runner, to ask her what the name of the tree was.

Off went the hare as fast as his legs could carry him and he found old Jemma in front of her hut.

"Oh, Mrs Jemma," he said. "We animals are dying of hunger. If you could only tell us the name of that wonderful tree of yours you could save us all from starving."

"Gladly I will do that," answered Jemma. "It's perfectly safe to eat the fruit. Its name is OSSOPIT."

"Oh," said the hare, "that's a very difficult name. I shall forget it by the time I get back."

"No, it's really quite easy," said Jemma. "Just think of 'opposite' and then sort of say it backwards, like this:

opposite — OSSOPIT."

"Oh, thanks very much," said the hare, and off he scampered.

As he ran he kept muttering, "opposite, ottipis, ossipit" and got all mixed up. So that when he got back to the other animals all he could say was, "Well, Jemma did tell me the name but I can't remember whether it's ossipit, ottipis, or ossupit. I do know it's got something to do with 'opposite'."

"Oh dear," they all sighed. "We had better send someone with a better memory."

"I'll go," said the goat. "I never forget anything." So he headed straight for Jemma's hut, grunting and snorting all the way.

"I'm sorry to bother you again, Mrs Jemma," he panted, "but that stupid hare couldn't remember the name of the tree. Do you mind telling it me once more?"

"Gladly I will," replied the old woman. "It's OSSOPIT. Just think of 'opposite' and then sort of say it backwards:

opposite — OSSOPIT."

"Rightee-oh," said the goat, "and thank you very much, I'm sure."

And off he galloped, fast as he could, kicking up clouds of dust, and all the way he kept saying: "ottopis, oppossit, possitto, otto . . ." until he got back.

"I know the name of that tree," he said. "It's oppitis, n . . . no . . . ossipit, n . . . no . . . otup . . . oh dear . . . I just can't get it right."

"Well, who can we send this time?" they all asked. They didn't want to bother old Jemma again.

"I'm perfectly willing to have a go," piped up a young sparrow. "I'll be back in no time," and with a whisk of his tail he had flown off before anyone could stop him.

"Good morrow, gentle Jemma," he said. "Could you please tell me the name of that tree just *once* more. Hare and goat just could *not* get it right."

"Right gladly I will," said old Jemma patiently. "It's OSSOPIT, OSS-O-PIT. It's a wee bit difficult but just think of 'opposite' and then sort of say it backwards:

opposite—OSSOPIT."

37

"I'm most grateful, madam," said the sparrow and flew off twittering to himself: "opposite, ossitup, ottupus, oissopit," until he finally got back to his famishing friends.

"Do tell us, sparrow," they all cried.

"Yes," chirped the sparrow. "It's definitely 'ossitup', n . . . no . . . oittusip, n . . . no . . . oippisuit . . . Oh dear, I give up. So very sorry."

By now the animals were desperate. Just imagine them all sitting round the gorgeous tree and unable to pick any of its mouth-watering fruit.

Suddenly up spoke the tortoise. "I shall go," he said. "I know it will take a bit of time but I will not forget the name once I've been told. My family has the finest reputation in the world for good memories."

"No," they moaned. "You are too slow. We shall all be dead by the time you get back."

"Why not let me take tortoise on my back?" asked the zebra. "I'm hopeless at remembering things but my speed is second to none. I'll have him back here in no time at all." They all

thought this was a splendid idea and so off raced the zebra with the tortoise clinging to his back.

"Good morning, Madam Jemma," said the tortoise. "I'm sorry I have no time to alight. But if we don't get the name of that tree most of us will be dead by tonight. That's why I've come on zebra's back. He's a bit faster than I am, you know."

"Yes, I rather think he is," smiled old Jemma benignly. "Well, it's OSSOPIT. Just think of 'opposite' and then sort of say it backwards, like this: opposite – OSS-O-PIT."

"Just let me repeat it three times before I go," said the tortoise, "just to see if I get it right." And then he said it, very, very slowly, deliberately and loudly, and nodding his tiny head at each syllable:

"OSS-O-PIT   OSS-O-PIT   OSS-O-PIT."

39

"Bravo!" said Jemma, "you'll never forget it now."

And she was right.

The zebra thudded back hot foot and the tortoise was never in any doubt that he had the name right at last.

"It's OSS-O-PIT," he announced to his ravenous friends.

"Ossopit, ossopit, ossopit," they all cried. "It's an ossopit tree, and it's perfectly safe to eat." And they all helped themselves to the wonderful fruit. You just can't imagine how delicious it tasted.

And to show how grateful they were, they appointed the tortoise their Chief Adviser on Important Matters (he has C.A.I.M. after his name). And he still is Chief Adviser to this very day.

MONKEYING ABOUT   Stephen Corrin

"Caps for sale! Caps for sale!" shouted the pedlar as he walked through the streets.

But where were the caps?

Not on a cart, not on a barrow, not on a sack on his back, not even on a tray strapped to his shoulders. This pedlar carried his caps, every single one of them, in an enormously high pile on the top of his own flat cap – on the top of his head.

First came the blue caps, on top of these the yellow caps, then the orange ones, then purple ones and then, on the very top of all, the bright red ones. The pedlar, of course, had to walk very straight and carefully so as not to spill the caps.

Usually the pedlar did quite a good trade, for people were amused by the way he walked and by the clever way he could pick out any colour a customer chose without even looking up or upsetting the pile. What happened was he used a special little stick with a flat top and, with this in his left hand, he held the whole pile balanced while his right hand skilfully whisked out the colour required. His right hand seemed able to stretch very high up indeed!

One day, however, for some odd reason, not a single person came out to buy a cap. The pedlar walked up and down the streets, back and forth, back and forth, shouting, "Caps for sale! Caps for sale!" at the top of his voice – but there were no customers.

At last the pedlar thought to himself, "Well, one gets good days and one gets bad days. Anyway, this will be a good chance for me to take a rest and enjoy a snooze in the fresh country air."

So off he set to a nearby wood.

He sat himself down very carefully, leaning his back against the trunk of a stout oak tree, and within seconds, believe it or not, he was fast asleep in the warm sunshine, the caps still piled high on his head.

How long he slept he had no idea, but when he awoke he straightaway put up his hand to feel for his caps. Strange to relate, only his own flat cap was there. What a shock!

He looked to his left. No caps.

He looked to his right. No caps.

He looked behind. No caps.

And, of course, he looked in front. No caps.

So he stood up and walked round and round the tree but – still no caps.

Then he looked up into the branches of the tree above him and – just try to guess what he saw: monkeys, monkeys, monkeys and monkeys, chattering their heads off and laughing with great glee. AND EVERY MONKEY HAD A CAP ON HIS HEAD.

Some had a red cap on,
some a yellow one,
some an orange one,
some a blue one
and some a purple one.

"Hey, you monkeys! Give me back my caps!" shouted the pedlar, shaking his fist at them. But the monkeys only shook their fists back at him, chuckling, "Tseek, tseek, tseek" and "Hee, hee, hee!"

"You cheeky rascals!" he shouted again. "Give me my caps back at once!" But the monkeys only continued their "tseek, tseek, tseek" and "hee, hee, hee". They seemed to be enjoying the fun hugely. The pedlar shouted himself hoarse and shook both his fists at them, but the monkeys only shook *their* fists back at him and tseek, tseek tseeked and hee, hee, hee'd for all their worth.

By now the pedlar was almost beside himself with rage. He stamped his foot and screamed, "You give me back my caps or else . . .!"

But the monkeys only stamped *their* feet back at him.

At his wits' end the pedlar took off his own flat cap and flung it to the ground, helpless with anger and impatience. And just as he was about to walk away, the monkeys DID EXACTLY AS HE HAD DONE. Each one pulled off the cap he was wearing and threw it to the ground. Down came all the caps – yellow, orange, blue, purple and red – scattered all over the place. What copy-cats! Or should we say, what copy-monkeys!

The pedlar picked them all up, one by one, and placed them on top of his own flat cap as before – the blue, the yellow, the orange, the purple and the bright red. He then walked back into the town, up and down the streets, merrily shouting, "Caps for sale! Caps for sale!" And this time he was lucky.

He sold the lot.

THE THREE LITTLE PIGS Traditional

Once upon a time three little pigs set out to seek their fortune.

The first little pig met a man with a bundle of straw, and said to him, "Please, man, give me some straw so that I can build a house with it." The man did, and the little pig built a house with it. Presently came along a wolf, and knocked at the door, and said, "Little pig, little pig, let me come in."

To which the pig answered, "No, no, by the hair of my chinny chin chin."

"Then I'll huff and I'll puff, and I'll blow your house in!" said the wolf. So he huffed and he puffed, and he blew his house in, and ate up the little pig.

46

The second pig met a man with a bundle of sticks and said, "Please, man, give me some sticks to build a house with"; which the man did, and the pig built his house.

Then along came the wolf and said, "Little pig, little pig, let me come in."

"No, no, by the hair of my chinny chin chin."

"Then I'll puff and I'll huff, and I'll blow your house in!" So he huffed and he puffed, and he puffed and he huffed, and at last he blew the house down, and ate up the second pig.

The third little pig met a man with a load of bricks, and said, "Please, man, give me some bricks to build a house with"; so the man gave him some bricks, and he built his house with them. Then the wolf came, as he did to the other little pigs, and said, "Little pig, little pig, let me come in."

"No, no, by the hair of my chinny chin chin."

"Then I'll huff and I'll puff, and I'll blow your house in."

Well, he huffed and he puffed, and he huffed and he puffed, and he puffed and he huffed; but he could *not* blow the house down. When he found that he could not, with all his huffing and puffing, he said, "Little pig, I know where there is a nice field of turnips."

"Where?" said the little pig.

"Oh, in Mr Smith's field; and if you will be ready tomorrow morning, I will call for you, and we will go together and get some for dinner."

"Very well," said the little pig. "I will be ready. What time do you mean to go?"

"Oh, at six o'clock."

Well, the little pig got up at five, and got the turnips and was home again before six. When the wolf came he said, "Little pig, are you ready?"

"Ready?" said the little pig. "I have been and come back again, and got a nice pot-full for dinner."

The wolf felt very angry at this, but thought that he would catch the little pig next time; so he said, "Little pig, I know where there is a nice apple-tree."

"Where?" said the pig.

"Down at Merry-Garden," replied the wolf. "I will come for you at five o'clock to-morrow, and we will go together and get some apples."

Well, the little pig woke at four the next morning, and bustled up, and went off for the apples, hoping to get back before the wolf came; but this time he had further to go, and had to climb a tree. Just as he was coming down from it, he saw the wolf coming. When the wolf came up he said, "Little pig! Are you here before me? Are they nice apples?"

"Yes, very," said the little pig. "I will throw you down one." And he threw it so far that, while the wolf had gone to fetch it, the little pig jumped down and ran home.

The next day the wolf came again, and said to the little pig, "Little pig, there is a fair in the town this afternoon: will you come with me?"

"Oh, yes," said the pig, "I will come; what time shall you be ready?"

"At three," said the wolf.

So the little pig went early again and got to the fair, and bought a butter churn, and was on his way home with it when he saw the wolf coming. So he got into the churn to hide, and rolled down the hill inside it, which frightened the wolf so much that he ran home without going to the fair.

He went to the little pig's house, and told him how frightened he had been by a great round thing which came down the hill past him.

Then the little pig said, "Hah! I frightened you, did I? I had been to the fair and bought a butter churn, and when I saw you I got into it, and rolled down the hill."

Then the wolf was very angry indeed, and declared he *would* eat up the little pig, and that he would get down the chimney after him.

But the little pig boiled a pot full of water, over the fire, and, just as the wolf was coming down, took off the cover of the pot, and in fell the wolf. Then the little pig boiled him up, and ate him for supper, and lived happy ever after.

56

THE CLEVER FOX   Traditional

Father Fox thought he was very clever. He lived with his wife and children near the forest. The five fox cubs were as beautiful as their parents, but they were always hungry. And Mother and Father Fox had to find them food.

One night they were coming home with food for their children.

"You know, our children are all so clever and so beautiful, I think they must take after me," said Father Fox.

"Don't talk so loudly or Tiger will hear you," answered his wife.

"Well, if Tiger does hear me, I am far too clever to let him catch us. You might not escape him alone, my dear, but my cleverness will do for both of us."

Just as he said this, they heard a growl in the darkness.

"Well, Father Fox, here I am, all ready to eat you both for my supper. Unless, of course, you're as clever as you say and can stop me?" And a large black and yellow Tiger stepped out of the bushes.

58

Father Fox was so upset and frightened that he could not speak. He had no idea what to do, for he wasn't really clever at all. He only *thought* he was clever.

Then Mother Fox said quietly:

"How lucky it is that we have met you, Uncle Tiger. You are so wise that I am sure you can answer a question that greatly worries us."

Now Tiger was vain, like Father Fox. He liked to be called wise. And to be called "Uncle" was a sign of great importance.

"Oh yes, I am sure I can help you. Hurry up with your question, then I will answer it before I eat you up."

"Well, Uncle," went on Mother Fox, "my husband and I
have five beautiful cubs. But we are not sure which are most
like my husband and which are most like me. You are so wise
that, if you looked at them, you could tell at once. Will you do
us this great honour?"

Tiger was very pleased about this. He thought to himself:
"I shall have five fat cubs for supper as well as these foolish
foxes." So he said:

"Lead the way to your home. Show me your cubs and I will
answer the question for you."

So the three of them went off together. When they came to

the fox hole leading to Fox's home, Mother Fox said:

"Now, husband, go down and tell the children of the great honour that clever Uncle Tiger is going to show them."

"Be quick," growled Tiger.

Father Fox *was* quick. He ran down the hole like a flash. Mother Fox and Tiger waited together by the hole.

But nobody came out, no Father Fox and no cubs.

Tiger was tired of waiting, he wanted his supper.

"Where is your husband? Where are the cubs?" he said.

"Uncle," answered Mother Fox, "if you'll excuse me, I will go and see."

61

"Tell them to be quick!"

"Yes, Uncle." And Mother Fox popped into the hole. Tiger sat and waited. He was angry. He was tired. And above all, he was hungry.

Then he saw Mother Fox's wise head and bright eyes, peeping at him from the hole.

"Oh, Uncle," she cried, "there is no need to trouble you after all. Father Fox has settled the question! He says the five cubs are all just like his clever and beautiful wife."

Tiger growled and tried to catch the fox with his paw. But she was too quick for him. She was gone in a flash.

Tiger had to go home to bed without any supper.

Father Fox stopped boasting about his cleverness. He knew now that his wife was the wise and clever one of the family.

THE HARE AND THE TORTOISE   Traditional

"I'm the fastest runner in the world," boasted Hare. "I can run faster than any other animal. I can move faster than any bird can fly."

The other animals agreed. It was much too hot to argue. Besides, Hare was very fast. There was no doubt about that. If only he wasn't so proud and pleased with himself. The other animals got very tired of hearing him boast. So they just nodded and agreed, and didn't pay much attention.

Hare turned to Tortoise, who was moving very slowly across the field, inch by inch. "Can't you go any faster?" Hare called. "How slowly you move!"

Tortoise paid no attention to Hare. He just kept on plodding over the ground. And he remembered what his mother had told him: "Slow but sure – that's the way. We always get there, we tortoises do, even though we move slowly."

So he answered Hare quite calmly. "I don't need to run fast to escape from my enemies. I've a thick shell – I can tuck my head inside the shell and I'm quite safe."

"But you are so slow!" said Hare. "Look how long it takes you to cross the field. You're so stupid and clumsy!"

"All right," said Tortoise, who wasn't going to let Hare call him stupid and clumsy, "I'll give you a race. Let's start level and see who gets there first."

"A race! Did you say a race?" Hare laughed and laughed.

Some of the other animals had come to see what was happening.

"Go on, then," they said. "Let's see you race!"

"All right," said Hare when he had stopped laughing. "Where to?"

There was an old windmill several fields away. "See that?" said Tortoise. "Let's race to the windmill!"

One of the animals said, "I'll be the starter," and the others cheered. Two rabbits said they would hold the tape at the finish, and Fox said he would be the judge and see fair play.

So Tortoise set off, moving very slowly. "I don't need to start yet," said Hare. "It won't take me any time at all to reach

64

the windmill. I've time for a nap. Ah . . ." he yawned. It really was a very hot day.

So he folded his paws and lay down in the shade, and was soon fast asleep and dreaming.

"Slow but sure," murmured Tortoise to himself as he plodded his way across the first field

Hare woke up and blinked. Where was Tortoise? Ah, there he was. He hadn't crossed the first field. There was plenty of time.

"What about the race, Hare?" asked one or two animals who hadn't joined the others at the finishing line.

"Race?" yawned Hare. "What race? Don't worry, my friends," he said. "Lots of time yet." And he stretched himself out on the grass and was soon fast asleep again.

When at last he woke, it was evening, and the air was cool. "I must have slept for quite a time," he said to himself. He looked round. Where was everyone? Then he remembered the race.

He looked across the fields. Where was Tortoise? Then he saw him, far away in the distance. He had almost crossed the last field and wasn't far from the finishing point. "There he is!" said Hare. "Well, I never! Time to get my skates on." And he started running as fast as he could. But soon he began to puff and pant.

At the windmill, all the animals had now gathered on either side of the finishing tape, which was held by two young rabbits. "Come on, Tortoise," they all yelled. "Good old Tortoise! You'll make it!"

"Slow but sure," the tortoise repeated for the hundredth time. "Slow but sure," he told himself. He was nearly there.

"Faster! Faster!" Hare muttered. He raced across the first field, then the second field and now he began to cross the third field. But he wasn't as fit as he used to be and soon he became out of breath. "Faster! Faster!"

The badgers and rabbits and voles jumped up and down in their excitement. "It's going to be a close thing," said the water rat. "Come on, Tortoise, hurry!"

"Maybe a photo finish," said Fox importantly, looking at his stopwatch.

"Slow but sure," said Tortoise again. Behind the Tortoise,

Hare panted across the field. But it was too late. Tortoise was nearly at the tape.

The noise grew deafening. "Tor-toise! Tor-toise!" the animals chanted. "Hurrah! Come on, Tortoise!"

Tortoise reached the tape and fell over the finishing line, exhausted. He just lay there, while all around him, the other animals jumped up and down and cheered.

Twenty yards behind, Hare puffed towards the finishing line. Too late! "Course," he said, "I'd have made it easily. I'm much the faster . . . If it had been a proper race . . ." But no one was listening to him.

They all crowded round Tortoise. "No doubt about it," said Fox importantly. "Tortoise is the winner!"

"How did you do it?" A hedgehog who reported for the *Animal Times* was beside Tortoise, notebook in hand. "Anything you'd like to say to our readers?"

Tortoise opened his eyes. "Slow but sure," he gasped.

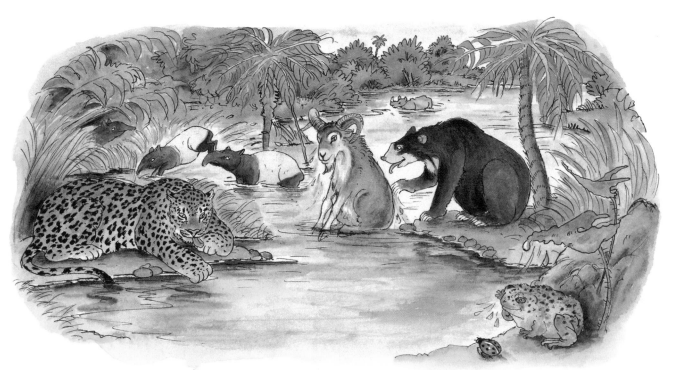

HOW THE POLAR BEAR BECAME   Ted Hughes

When the animals had been on earth for some time they grew
tired of admiring the trees, the flowers, and the sun. They
began to admire each other. Every animal was eager to be
admired, and spent a part of each day making itself look
more beautiful.

Soon they began to hold beauty contests.

Sometimes Tiger won the prize, sometimes Eagle, and
sometimes Ladybird. Every animal tried hard.

One animal in particular won the prize almost every time.
This was Polar Bear.

Polar Bear was white. Not quite snowy white, but much
whiter than any of the other creatures. Everyone admired her.
In secret, too, everyone was envious of her. But however much
they wished that she wasn't quite so beautiful, they couldn't
help giving her the prize.

70

"Polar Bear," they said, "with your white fur, you are almost too beautiful."

All this went to Polar Bear's head. In fact, she became vain. She was always washing and polishing her fur, trying to make it still whiter. After a while she was winning the prize every time. The only times any other creature got a chance to win was when it rained. On those days Polar Bear would say: "I shall not go out in the wet. The other creatures will be muddy, and my white fur may get splashed."

Then perhaps, Frog or Duck would win for a change.

She had a crowd of young admirers who were always hanging around her cave. They were mainly Seals, all very giddy. Whenever she came out they made a loud shrieking roar: "Ooooooh! How beautiful she is!"

Before long, her white fur was more important to Polar Bear than anything. Whenever a single speck of dust landed on the tip of one hair of it – she was furious.

"How can I be expected to keep beautiful in this country!" she cried then. "None of you have ever seen me at my best, because of the dirt here. I am really much whiter than any of you have ever seen me. I think I shall have to go into another country. A country where there is none of this dust. Which country would be best?"

She used to talk in this way because then the Seals would cry: "Oh, please don't leave us. Please don't take your beauty away from us. We will do anything for you."

And she loved to hear this.

Soon animals were coming from all over the world to look at her. They stared and stared as Polar Bear stretched out on her rock in the sun.

Then they went off home and tried to make themselves look like her. But it was no use. They were all the wrong colour. They were black,

or brown,

or yellow,

or ginger,

or fawn,

or speckled, but not one of them was white.

Soon most of them gave up trying to look beautiful. But they still came every day to gaze enviously at Polar Bear. Some brought picnics. They sat in a vast crowd among the trees in front of her cave.

"Just look at her," said Mother Hippo to her children. "Now see that you grow up like that."

But nothing pleased Polar Bear.

"The dust these crowds raise!" she sighed. "Why can't I ever get away from them? If only there were some spotless, shining country, all for me . . ."

Now pretty well all the creatures were tired of her being so much more admired than they were. But one creature more so than the rest. Peregrine Falcon.

He was a beautiful bird, all right. But he was not white. Time and again, in the beauty contest he was runner-up to Polar Bear.

"If it were not for her," he raged to himself, "I should be first every time."

He thought and thought for a plan to get rid of her. How? How? How? At last he had it.

One day he went up to Polar Bear.

Now Peregrine Falcon had been to every country in the world. He was a great traveller, as all the creatures well knew.

"I know a country," he said to Polar Bear, "which is so clean it is even whiter than you are. Yes, yes, I know you are beautifully white, but this country is even whiter. The rocks are clean glass and the earth is frozen ice-cream. There is no dirt there, no dust, no mud. You would become whiter than ever in that country. And no one lives there. You could be queen of it."

Polar Bear tried to hide her excitement.

"I could be queen of it, you say?" she cried. "This country sounds made for me. No crowds, no dirt? And the rocks, you say, are glass?"

"The rocks," said Peregrine Falcon, "are mirrors."

"Wonderful!" cried Polar Bear.

"And the rain," he said, "is white face powder."

"Better than ever!" she cried. "How quickly can I be there, away from all these staring crowds and all this dirt? I am going to another country," she told the other animals. "It is too dirty here to live."

Peregrine Falcon hired Whale to carry his passenger. He sat on Whale's forehead, calling out the directions. Polar Bear sat on the shoulder, gazing at the sea. The Seals, who had begged to go with her, sat on the tail.

After some days, they came to the North Pole, where it is all snow and ice.

"Here you are," cried Peregrine Falcon. "Everything just as I said. No crowds, no dirt, nothing but beautiful clean whiteness."

"And the rocks actually are mirrors!" cried Polar Bear, and she ran to the nearest iceberg to repair her beauty after the long trip.

Every day now, she sat on one iceberg or another, making herself beautiful in the mirror of the ice. Always, near her, sat the Seals. Her fur became whiter and whiter in this new clean country. And as it became whiter, the Seals praised her beauty more and more. When she herself saw the improvement in her looks she said: "I shall never go back to that dirty old country again."

And there she is still, with all her admirers around her.

Peregrine Falcon flew back to the other creatures and told them that Polar Bear had gone for ever. They were all very glad, and set about making themselves beautiful at once. Every single one was saying to himself: "Now that Polar Bear is out of the way, perhaps I shall have a chance of the prize at the beauty contest."

And Peregrine Falcon was saying to himself: "Surely, now, I am the most beautiful of all creatures."

But that first contest was won by Little Brown Mouse for her pink feet.

THE SHOOTING   Roald Dahl

"Well, my darling," said Mr Fox. "What shall it be tonight?"

"I think we'll have duck tonight," said Mrs Fox. "Bring us two fat ducks, if you please. One for you and me, and one for the children."

"Ducks it shall be!" said Mr Fox. "Bunce's best!"

"Now do be careful," said Mrs Fox.

"My darling," said Mr Fox, "I can smell those goons a mile away. I can even smell one from the other. Boggis gives off a filthy stink of rotten chicken-skins. Bunce reeks of goose-livers, and as for Bean, the fumes of apple cider hang around him like poisonous gases."

80

"Yes, but just don't get careless," said Mrs Fox. "You know they'll be waiting for you, all three of them."

"Don't you worry about me," said Mr Fox. "I'll see you later."

But Mr Fox would not have been quite so cocky had he known exactly *where* the three farmers were waiting at that moment. They were just outside the entrance to the hole, each one crouching behind a tree with his gun loaded. And what is more, they had chosen their positions very carefully, making sure that the wind was not blowing from them towards the fox's hole. In fact, it was blowing in the opposite direction. There was no chance of them being 'smelled out'.

Mr Fox crept up the dark tunnel to the mouth of his hole. He poked his long handsome face out into the night air and sniffed once.

He moved an inch or two forward and stopped.

He sniffed again. He was always especially careful when coming out from his hole.

He inched forward a little more. The front half of his body was now in the open.

82

His black nose twitched from side to side, sniffing and
sniffing for the scent of danger. He found none, and he was just
about to go trotting forward into the wood when he heard or
thought he heard a tiny noise, a soft rustling sound, as though
someone had moved a foot ever so gently through a patch of
dry leaves.

Mr Fox flattened his body against the ground and lay very
still, his ears pricked. He waited a long time, but he heard
nothing more.

"It must have been a field-mouse," he told himself, "or some
other small animal."

He crept a little further out of the hole . . . then further still. He was almost right out in the open now. He took a last careful look around. The wood was murky and very still. Somewhere in the sky the moon was shining.

Just then, his sharp night-eyes caught a glint of something bright behind a tree not far away. It was a small silver speck of moonlight shining on a polished surface. Mr Fox lay still, watching it. What on earth was it? Now it was moving. It was coming up and up . . . *Great heavens! It was the barrel of a gun!*

Quick as a whip, Mr Fox jumped back into his hole and at that same instant the entire wood seemed to explode around him. *Bang-bang! Bang-bang! Bang-bang!*

The smoke from the three guns floated upward in the night air. Boggis and Bunce and Bean came out from behind their trees and walked towards the hole.

86

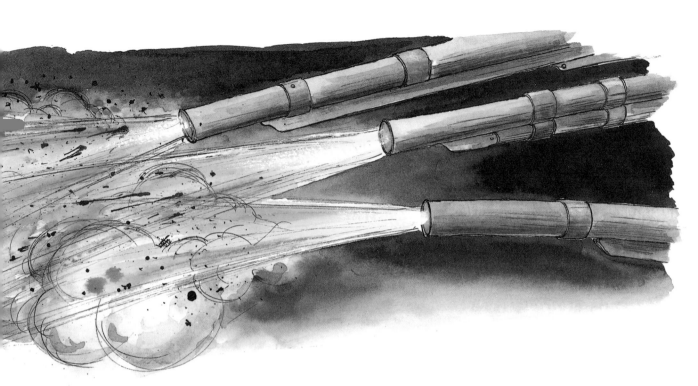

"Did we get him?" said Bean.

One of them shone a flashlight on the hole, and there on the ground, in the circle of light, half in and half out of the hole, lay the poor tattered bloodstained remains of . . . a fox's tail. Bean picked it up. "We got the tail but we missed the fox," he said, tossing the thing away.

"Dang and blast!" said Boggis. "We shot too late. We should have let fly the moment he poked his head out."

"He won't be poking it out again in a hurry," Bunce said.

Bean pulled a flask from his pocket and took a swig of cider. Then he said, "It'll take three days at least before he gets hungry enough to come out again. I'm not sitting around here waiting for that. Let's dig him out."

"Ah," said Boggis. "Now you're talking sense. We can dig him out in a couple of hours. We know he's there."

"I reckon there's a whole family of them down that hole," Bunce said.

"Then we'll have the lot," said Bean. "Get the shovels!"

***

Down in the hole, Mrs Fox was tenderly licking the stump of Mr Fox's tail to stop the bleeding. "It was the finest tail for miles around," she said between licks.

"It hurts," said Mr Fox.

"I know it does, sweetheart. But it'll soon get better."

"And it will soon grow again, Dad," said one of the Small Foxes.

"It will never grow again," said Mr Fox. "I shall be tail-less for the rest of my life." He looked very glum.

There was no food for the foxes that night, and soon the children dozed off. Then Mrs Fox dozed off. But Mr Fox couldn't sleep because of the pain in the stump of his tail. "Well," he thought, "I suppose I'm lucky to be alive at all. And now they've found our hole, we're going to have to move out as soon as possible. We'll never get any peace if we . . . What was *that*?"

He turned his head sharply and listened. The noise he heard now was the most frightening noise a fox can ever hear – the scrape-scrape-scraping of shovels digging into the soil.

"Wake up!" he shouted. "They're digging us out!"

Mrs Fox was wide awake in one second. She sat up, quivering all over. "Are you sure that's it?" she whispered.

"I'm positive! Listen!"

"They'll kill my children!" cried Mrs Fox.

"Never!" said Mr Fox.

"But darling, they will!" sobbed Mrs Fox. "You know they will!"

Scrunch, scrunch, scrunch went the shovels above their heads. Small stones and bits of earth began falling from the roof of the tunnel.

"How will they kill us, Mummy?" asked one of the small foxes. His round black eyes were huge with fright. "Will there be dogs?" he said.

Mrs Fox began to cry. She gathered her four children close to her and held them tight.

Suddenly there was an especially loud crunch above their heads and the sharp end of a shovel came right through the ceiling. The sight of this awful thing seemed to have an electric effect upon Mr Fox. He jumped up and shouted, "I've got it! Come on! There's not a moment to lose! Why didn't I think of it before!"

"Think of what, Dad?"

"A fox can dig quicker than a man!" shouted Mr Fox, beginning to dig. "Nobody in the world can dig as quick as a fox!"

The soil began to fly out furiously behind Mr Fox as he started to dig for dear life with his front feet. Mrs Fox ran forward to help him. So did the four children.

"Go downwards!" ordered Mr Fox. "We've got to go deep! As deep as we possibly can!"

The tunnel began to grow longer and longer. It sloped
steeply downward. Deeper and deeper below the surface of
the ground it went. The mother and the father and all four
of the children were digging together. Their front legs were
moving so fast you couldn't see them. And gradually the
scrunching and scraping of the shovels became fainter and
fainter.

After about an hour, Mr Fox stopped digging. "Hold it!" he
said. They all stopped. They turned and looked back up the

long tunnel they had just dug. All was quiet. "Phew!" said Mr Fox. "I think we've done it! They'll never get as deep as this. Well done everyone!"

They all sat down, panting for breath. And Mrs Fox said to her children, "I should like you to know that if it wasn't for your father we should all be dead by now. Your father is a fantastic fox."

Mr Fox looked at his wife and she smiled. He loved her more than ever when she said things like that.

DRAGONS AND GIANTS
Arnold Lobel

Frog and Toad were reading
a book together.
    "The people in this book are brave,"
said Toad. "They fight dragons
and giants, and they are never afraid."
    "I wonder if we are brave," said Frog.
    Frog and Toad looked into a mirror.
    "We look brave," said Frog.
    "Yes, but are we?" asked Toad.

Frog and Toad went outside.
"We can try to climb this mountain,"
said Frog. "That should tell us
if we are brave."
Frog went leaping over rocks,
and Toad came puffing up
behind him.

They came to a dark cave.
A big snake came out of the cave.
   "Hello, lunch," said the snake
when he saw Frog and Toad.
He opened his wide mouth.
   Frog and Toad jumped away.
Toad was shaking.
   "I am not afraid!" he cried.

They climbed higher, and they
heard a loud noise.

Many large stones were rolling down
the mountain.

"It's an avalanche!" cried Toad.

Frog and Toad jumped away.
Frog was trembling.

"I am not afraid!" he shouted.

They came to the top of the mountain.
The shadow of a hawk fell over them.
Frog and Toad jumped under a rock.
The hawk flew away.

"We are not afraid!" screamed Frog and
Toad at the same time.

Then they ran down the mountain
very fast.

They ran past the place where they saw
the avalanche.

They ran past the place where they saw
the snake.

They ran all the way to Toad's house.

"Frog, I am glad to have a brave friend like you," said Toad.

He jumped into the bed and pulled the covers over his head.

"And I am happy to know a brave person like you, Toad," said Frog.

He jumped into the cupboard and shut the door.

Toad stayed in the bed, and Frog stayed in the cupboard.

They stayed there for a long time, just feeling very brave together.

THE FRIENDLIEST DOG IN THE WORLD

Anne Forsyth

Oz was the friendliest dog in the world. He sat by the gate all day and everyone stopped to pat him.

Tim was proud of such a friendly dog. So when Dad came home with the news, "We're going to live in Scotland!", Tim said very firmly, "I'm not going without Oz."

"Of course he'll come too!" said Mum. "He's our dog."

Tim wasn't sure about going to Scotland. It was such a long distance from London. And people spoke in such a strange way.

It seemed even stranger when they arrived in Edinburgh – all tall grey buildings.

"You'll like it," said Mum, as they unpacked. "Wait till you start school. You'll soon make friends."

Tim felt really lost. He couldn't understand what people said, and he missed his friends. Oz sat at his feet as if he knew that Tim was unhappy.

And then – even worse – Oz disappeared. He raced through a gap in the hedge and was off. A few hours later, he came back, but not for long. As soon as Mum opened the door, he'd slip out and squeeze through the gap.

"I hope he doesn't get lost," said Tim.

The night watchman at the factory settled down by the fire. He had ham sandwiches for later, and a flask of tea. It was very snug inside the little hut.

Then he heard a clatter, as if someone had knocked over a dustbin lid.

"Got you!" He shone his torch at the burglar.

Only it wasn't a burglar, but a little black dog.

"Well!" said the watchman. "Come on in."

Oz – because that's who it was – didn't need to be asked twice.

"Would you like a bit of my sandwich?" asked the watchman.

Oz ate up every bit and settled down on an old rug.

When morning came, he barked at the door of the hut.

"Right," said the watchman. "Off you go home. Is there a name and address on your collar? Funny, that's not an address round here. You must be a stray."

Every night, Oz came to visit the watchman. "He's a real guard dog," the watchman said. "The least sound and he's out there. Don't know his name. I call him Paws."

That night he asked his wife to put in an extra bacon sandwich.

"Woof!" said Oz. Bacon sandwiches were his favourite.

The little primary school wasn't far from the factory. The children had gone out to play, and the dinner lady was clearing up. "Well!" she said. "We've got a visitor." She put some scraps of pie on a piece of newspaper and laid it at the kitchen door. "Good dog."

Oz – for that's who it was – ate up the scraps and followed her about until she shut the door firmly.

But next day he was back again. He pushed open the kitchen door and put on his pleading look. "You again!" said the dinner lady. "You're a comic. There – it's haggis today."

Oz had never eaten haggis. It was a kind of meat all chopped up and boiled in a skin. It smelt very tasty.

"I've never seen a dog eat so fast," said the dinner lady. "I'll call you Jaws." She looked at his collar. "I don't know where that is. Poor wee dog. You must be lost."

For a time, Oz sat on the wall and watched the children playing – then he joined in, chasing the ball with excited yelps. After that, he was off again – where next?

The old lady lived in a cottage near the school. She lived mostly in one room with old photographs and china and other treasures.

One day she was working in her garden and listening to a robin chirping. Suddenly something brushed against her legs and the robin flew away.

"Oh!" she said. "What a surprise!" She looked down at the small black dog. "Where did you come from?"

She looked at his collar. "You must be a stray. Poor thing. Come on in."

She opened a packet of biscuits and gave two to Oz, who gave her a paw in return.

Then he lay down by the fireside until it got dark, and he shook himself and wandered off into the night.

The old lady began to watch for Oz every afternoon. She would buy tins of dog food from the supermarket, and sometimes a bone from the butcher.

"It was going to be so dull this Christmas," she said. "But now you've come to visit me. I'll call you Santa Claus – Claus for short."

Tim was worried and so were Mum and Dad. What had happened to Oz? "We should have put his new address on his collar," said Mum.

"He'll turn up," said Dad.

"Let's put a notice in the newsagent's window," said Mum. So Tim wrote on a postcard:

LOST. Small black mongrel. Very friendly.

And he added his name and address.

Next day was Saturday. The dinner lady went into the newsagent's to pay for her newspapers. She glanced at the cards in the window, and stopped. "Lost," she said. "Well, I wonder. . . ."

The old lady went to the post office next door to buy stamps. It was busy, so she paused and looked in the window of the newsagent's.

"Lost . . ." She nodded. "Yes, very friendly. It could be . . ."

The watchman decided to buy a newspaper to read the football pages. He too stopped to look at the cards in the window.

"Well," he said. "That certainly sounds like my friend Paws."

"We're all feeling low today," said Mum. "I'll make a special cake for tea."

"Mmmm . . . that smells good," said Dad, as Mum took the cake from the oven. Just then, the doorbell rang.

"Excuse me," said the man on the doorstep. He had a cheerful red face. "Your phone's not working – did you know? I think I've seen your dog."

"Great!" said Dad.

At that moment, a woman jumped off her bicycle. "Hello!" she called. "I think I've seen your dog . . ."

"Great!" said Dad.

The man sat down and undid his muffler. "I'm a watchman," he said. "One night, I was sitting by the fire. Outside, it was pitch black and very spooky . . ."

Tim liked ghost stories that began like this – and the watchman enjoyed telling stories.

He'd just started when the bell rang again. There stood a very old lady.

"I think I've seen your dog," she said.

"Great!" said Dad.

The kitchen was quite crowded by now. "Just a moment," said Mum. "I hear something." She opened the kitchen door.

"Paws!"

"Jaws!"

"Claus!"

"Oz!" shouted Tim. Oz jumped up and down and wagged his tail.

110

"I think," said Mum, smiling, "we should all have a cup of tea."

Soon the watchman was telling stories about the town. And the old lady hadn't talked so much for ages.

The dinner lady asked Tim where he went to school. "Do you know my Jamie? I'll bring him round tomorrow."

Tim began to cheer up. Maybe he'd make friends after all.

"Such a gentle dog," said the old lady.

"Proper comic," said the dinner lady.

"Brave wee dog," said the watchman.

"That doesn't sound like our Oz," said Dad.

They all turned to look at Oz, but he wasn't there.

"He's gone exploring again," said Mum. "And when he comes back, we'll get his new address put on his collar. No wonder he ran away."

"This is his home now," said Tim.

"That's right," said Mum. "More cake, anyone?"

TIM RABBIT'S PARTY   Alison Uttley

Such a rubbing and a scrubbing was going on under the ground, in the little cottage where Tim Rabbit lived! Such a dusting and a cleaning and a polishing of the candle-sticks and the pepper-pot and saucepans! Mrs Rabbit's kitchen was shining with all the little bright things you can imagine.

Little brass mirrors hung on the wall, copper pans were ranged on the shelf round the room. In small hollows were glow-worms, shining with their own green light. Hanging from the ceiling were bunches of rosemary and thyme and lavender, sending out sweet smells. The ground was covered with a new carpet of wild flowers, tiny blue and white blossoms with petals like silk.

Mr Rabbit was walking up and down giving the final touches. Mrs Rabbit was cooking the buns and cakes, piling them on dishes. Tim was darting in and out carrying jugs of spring water, for lemonade and ginger-beer, although of course it wasn't ordinary lemonade and ginger-beer. No, the lemonade was made of honey and rose leaves with a pinch of lemon balm, and the ginger-beer was made of the hot flowers of snapdragon and dandelion.

Whatever was all this excitement for? It was Tim Rabbit's birthday and he was having his first real party. All his school friends were coming. Old Jonathan had given them a holiday. Seven little school mates would be there, all except one belonging to the famous family of Rabbit – Adam and Bill Rabbit from Nettle Lane, Charlie and Don from Tansy Common, Fanny and Kate from Daisy Dell, and last of all, little Sam Hare.

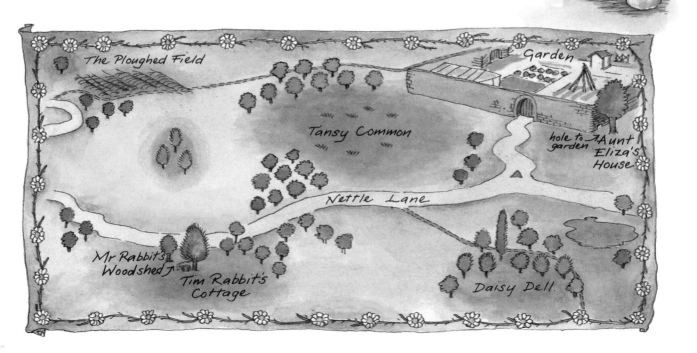

"Wherever shall we put them all?" asked Mrs Rabbit. "There won't be room to sit down!"

"We don't want to sit," said Tim, quickly.

"I mean your father and me to sit down," said Mrs Rabbit. "We shall want to rest our old bones."

"Oh, I shan't be here," said Mr Rabbit quietly. "I can't stand the clatter of all that crowd. I shall go out to the woodshed to do a bit of carpentry."

"Well, Father. I shall be sorry to miss you, but you would be rather in the way," said Tim, politely.

"Hum," grunted Mr Rabbit, rather crossly. "I shall make a rabbit hutch if you're not careful, Tim."

"Cakes, sandwiches, buns, pasties," said Mrs Rabbit, running to the table from the pantry and putting out the plates of good things. "Wild thyme buns, and saffron buns. Sage cheeses and crab-apple pasty. Egg and sorrel sandwiches. Dandelion slices. All fit for the King of England himself, bless him."

"Cherry jam and sloe jam. Hawthorn jelly and rose-hip jelly," said little Tim, dancing round the table, and looking at the white pots, each with a wooden spoon at its side, and a cap of green leaf covering it.

Mr Rabbit opened the door of the medicine cupboard in the wall. "Wormwood tea, rue tea, bittersweet mixture, castor oil and weasel-snout ointment. That's what you will want if you eat all this," said he, and his eyes twinkled at little Tim.

"We haven't any lettuces," cried Tim suddenly. "I'm going to get some. I know where they grow. In Aunt Eliza's garden."

"It isn't safe there, Tim. Aunt Eliza seldom goes in her garden. There's a new gardener, a very spry young man."

"I don't care a pin for the new gardener," said Tim, throwing back his head proudly.

"Now Tim! Don't boast. We have enough without lettuces. Go out and gather a bunch of flowers for the centre of the table. Be quick. They are coming at three o'clock."

Tim ran off, but he had made up his mind to get the lettuce.

"Lettuce?" said Aunt Eliza, when Tim knocked at her door and scampered in to the little house by the garden. "There's a new gardener, not like the old, deaf, sleepy one. I haven't been since he came. I was warned!"

"I don't care a pin for the new gardener," said Tim. "It's for my birthday party, Aunt Eliza."

"Well! Well! I'll find a birthday present for you, and be quick back, Tim. Don't dawdle or he may catch you."

Tim went through the hole in the wall, that was Aunt Eliza's private doorway. Oh dear! He was caught in a net spread across the opening. He dashed right into it, and it wrapped itself round him. He was frightened, poor little Tim! He could hear the gardener digging in the distance, and the birds singing in the trees over his head.

"Poor Tim Rabbit! Caught at last!" they sang.

"There's nobody to set him free!" called the Wood-pigeons.

"What shall we do?" asked the Thrush. "What shall we do?"

"Let him go! Let him go!" cooed a Dove.

"You'll catch it! You'll catch it!" mocked the Magpies.

Everybody seemed to be talking and giving advice to poor little Tim Rabbit, who lay there in the net.

The gardener looked at the birds, listened a moment, and stuck his fork in the ground.

"Something going on to make those birds chatter," said he, and he strode across the vegetable beds.

"So, I've cotched you, young varmint," said he, and he lifted Tim up by the ears and looked at him closely.

"Please, sir – please, sir –" stuttered Tim.

"What was ye after? Eh?" asked the gardener.

"A lettuce for my birthday party," stammered Tim. It was difficult to speak with one's ears held up.

"A lettuce? A birthday party?" said the gardener, and he scratched his head, but he didn't let Tim go.

"Yes, sir," said Tim, faintly.

"Are ye any relation of Tim Rabbit?" asked the gardener, and he actually smiled at Tim.

"I am Tim Rabbit, sir. I am Tim. I am him. I am Tim. I am," said Tim quickly.

"Then if so be ye are that selfsame Rabbit, I've a mind to –"

"What?" asked Tim, as the man hesitated.

"To take ye home with me. For my own children have heard of ye. They'll want to see ye. They told me to keep my eyes open for a bunny in a blue coat."

"Please, sir, if you'll let me go, I'll tell your children a tale. Yes, I will," cried Tim.

"Nay, I'll take ye home first," said the gardener. He stuffed Tim in his pocket, but Tim gave a leap and out he jumped. Away across the garden he scuttered and the gardener ran after him.

"Can't stop!" cried Tim, squeezing under the gate. "I shall be late for my party."

The gardener laughed and threw a lettuce over the garden wall.

"Take your lettuce, Tim Rabbit, and mind ye come to my cottage one night soon and tell a tale to my little ones."

"I won't forget," promised Tim. He picked up the lettuce and ran back to Aunt Eliza.

"Oh, Tim, I thought you was cotched," she cried.

"Yes. I was, but he let me go," answered Tim. "Have you got my present, Aunt Eliza?"

"Here it is, Tim." Aunt Eliza held out a bit of looking-glass she had found in the wood. Tim could see his nose and his whiskers in it. It was a really wonderful present, and Tim hugged his Aunt Eliza as he thanked her.

Then away he ran home. The guests were already straggling along the paths, one behind another. Six little rabbits and Sam Hare dawdling along at the end. Tim dashed through the bushes and got home first.

"They're coming! They'll be here in a minute," he cried, and he washed his dirty hands and brushed his hair before his own looking-glass just in time.

The company came up to the door. Pit! pat! they came. They tapped and giggled, and shuffled on their soft feet, and whispered as they rapped on the door.

When Mrs Rabbit opened to them, they crowded in, filling the room, and Mr Rabbit sidled out of the back door.

"We've brought you some presents,

Tim. Many happy returns of the day," they said, and they held out their gifts.

A string-bag, but of course it wasn't made of string, but of horsehair, from Adam Rabbit.

A piece of honeycomb from the wild bees' nest, from Bill.

A book made of nut leaves sewn together, but there was no printing in it, from Charlie.

A ball, not made of rubber, but of cowslips, from Don.

A purse, not made of leather, but of puffball skin, from Fanny.

A set of ninepins, but they were really fir cones, from Kate.

A lovely red pincushion, but it was a robin's pincushion from a rose bush, from Sam Hare.

"Thank you! Thank you! Thank you!" cried Tim with delight as he took the presents from his friends.

First of all they had tea, and they ate everything up, so that the plates were quite clean at the end of the feast.

Then they played games, for the table was moved away into the field to make more room. They played postman's knock. Each one tapped at the little green door just like a real postman, but of course they brought rabbit-kisses in their bags, not real kisses. You know what rabbit-kisses are, don't you? Rabbits rub their little soft noses when they kiss.

They played musical chairs, but they had no chairs, for Mrs Rabbit was sitting on the only one. The music came from a wheat-stalk pipe, that she played to keep them running.

119

They danced, but their dance wasn't a waltz or even a polka. It was a Bunny-trot, which is quite fun to dance. There was no band, but a nightingale and a thrush and a blackbird in the little wood close to the door sang their sweetest for the company.

They pulled crackers, but they were not the crackers you know, made of coloured paper and tinsel with a bang and a toy inside. The crackers were the long seed-cases of the balsam, that go off like a fairy gun when anyone touches them. They had great fun with these.

They rang hand-bells and played a tune, but the bells were not those you play. They were harebells from the fields.

They played hide the thimble, and even that was different, for Mrs Rabbit's thimble was a foxglove flower which she put on her paw when she did the mending.

All the time they played they could hear a little tap, tap, tap going on outside in the woodshed.

"What's that noise? Is it a woodpecker?" asked little Adam Rabbit.

"It's Father doing his carpentry," said Tim. "He likes tapping."

So on they went, and they made such a racket that even the tap-tap of Mr Rabbit's hammer could hardly be heard.

They said good-bye and went off down the garden path, calling "Good-bye" and "Thank you very much," but still the tap-tapping went on.

120

"They've all gone now and it's been a lovely party," called Tim at the keyhole. "Come out, Father."

"I can't! I've been hammering all this time to tell you I'm fastened in," cried Mr Rabbit, and his voice sounded very cross indeed. "Why didn't you come before?"

"We thought you were working, Father," stammered Tim. He shook the door and ran in to the kitchen to call his mother.

"Father's stuck!" he cried. "He can't get out."

Mrs Rabbit pulled, Mr Rabbit banged with his hammer. The little door of the woodshed was fast as if it had been glued.

"It's locked, and the key's gone," said Mrs Rabbit.

"Somebody's gone and fastened you in, Father," shouted Tim.

"I know that. I guessed as much two hours ago," grunted Mr Rabbit. "I'm hungry and here I'm stuck."

"Who can have done it?" whispered Tim to his mother.

In his heart he knew. It was little Sam Hare, of course. Sam didn't care a brass button for anybody. Sam had gone out of the room for postman's knock, and when they called he came in with a sly look on his face.

"Who can have done it?" whispered Mrs Rabbit to Tim.

"Never mind who done it or who didn't done it, it's done and I'm nearly done," groaned poor Mr Rabbit, whose hearing was sharper than they had imagined.

So Tim and Mrs Rabbit pushed and banged, and Mr Rabbit hammered and stamped, but the little door was made of sturdy oak, and what could three little rabbits with their soft paws and a small hammer do? The woodshed was far older and stronger than the house they lived in.

"Somebody's got the key," said Mrs Rabbit.

"Of course they have," shouted Mr Rabbit. "You would have unlocked it if the key was there, wouldn't you?"

"Don't shout, my dear," said Mrs Rabbit. "The neighbours will think we are quarrelling, and we never quarrel."

"We shall quarrel now if I don't get out," roared Mr Rabbit. "I'm hungry."

"We can feed you through the keyhole," said Tim, hopefully.

"I won't be fed through the keyhole," shouted Mr Rabbit.

"You can only pour soup through a keyhole, Tim," said Mrs Rabbit sadly.

"I don't like soup," roared Mr Rabbit.

"I'll go and look for a key," said Tim.

He brought the key of the cuckoo-clock, and the key of the money-box, but they wouldn't open the door. He brought the wooden spoon and the silver salt spoon, but they wouldn't unlock the door.

"I'll find Sam Hare and give him what for, locking up my father," said Tim to himself.

"I'll go and look for the key, Mother," he said aloud. "I 'specks it's somewhere about."

Out in the ploughed field little Sam Hare was leaping and dancing with delight. He was singing a ditty, and the words came faintly to Tim as he raced towards his friend.

"One, two, three.
I found a little key.
I put it in a wooden box,
And hid it in a tree.

"One, two, three.
I've lost my little key.
I threw it down a dark hole,
And now it's hid from me."

123

"Where's that key, Sam? You took it. What have you done with it?" shouted Tim.

"I've lost it. Can't 'member where I threw it," said Sam, and he turned head over heels. He was madly dancing in the wind.

"My dad's as cross as two sticks," remarked Tim.

"Is he?" Sam was surprised. "I thought he would laugh."

"He's hungry. He wants to come out," said Tim, solemnly.

"I never thought of that. I'll try to find it, Tim."

Together they ran in and out of the trees, looking for a hole. It is astonishing what a number of holes and hiding-places there are in a wood. Every tree has a cupboard where a Hare may hide a tiny iron key.

"It's like hunt the thimble," said Sam Hare. There was a scutter of feet and the rest of the party came to join them. Eight little animals, all hunted here and there in the wood, and at last there was a shout of joy. Little Adam Rabbit found the key, shut in its walnut-shell box, put tidily in a hole in the beech tree's roots.

124

When Tim got home he found poor Mrs Rabbit fast asleep on the doormat, and Mr Rabbit's snores came from the woodshed.

Tim unlocked the door and awoke his father.

"Is that you, Tim?" yawned Mr Rabbit. "Did you find the key?"

"Yes, Father. It was in a beech tree," said Tim demurely.

"Very strange. Very strange that the key of our woodshed should get in a tree," said Mr Rabbit, as he walked out of his prison.

"There are strange things in the world," said Mrs Rabbit. "I'm glad we have No Ordinary Rabbit to find our lost key."

Tim coughed and blushed. They went indoors and soon Mr Rabbit was eating his hot posset, and hearing all about the party.

"I promised to go to the gardener's cottage and tell a tale to his children," said Tim.

"Tell them about me being locked up by little Sam Hare," said Mr Rabbit.

"How did you know?" cried Tim.

"That would be telling," said Mr Rabbit softly, and that was all they could get out of him.

So the next night Tim went to the cottage and sat outside the window. He told his tale to the gardener's little children, but what he said must wait for another time.

126

THE PROUD AND FEARLESS LION

Ann and Reg Cartwright

Once there was a proud and fearless lion. Every morning he would go into the jungle and roar his mighty roar. So terrifying was this roar that all the animals would run away and hide; and so loud was this roar that the ground would shake and the leaves would fall from the trees.

"That'll show 'em who's boss!" said the proud and fearless lion.

One night word went round the jungle that it would rain. "There will be a great storm," said the little mouse. "We must all take shelter."

The big animals sheltered in a cave, the smaller ones in holes in the ground, and the birds snuggled together in the trees.

"Pooh!" said the proud and fearless lion. "A little rain never hurt anyone." And just to show how proud and fearless he was, he climbed to the top of his favourite hill and went to sleep. All night long it rained and rained, but on he slept.

The next morning the rain had stopped and the jungle was unusually quiet. Mouse woke up, sniffed the air and listened for Lion's roar. But for the first time ever it did not come.

That's strange, thought Mouse.

One by one the animals emerged, and because there was no sign of Lion they were not afraid. Mouse was curious to discover what had happened to Lion.

"I think we should go and search for him," she squeaked.

"Whatever for?" grumbled Giraffe. "He's always been a show-off, roaring and frightening us."

129

130

"I know he makes a lot of noise," said Mouse. "But has he ever hurt you?"

The animals had to agree that Lion had never hurt anyone.

So the animals set off to look for Lion. They found him on top of his hill. He opened his mouth to roar, but only a little squeak came out, followed by ATISHOO! He was no longer a proud and fearless lion – just a soggy, saggy, snivelling lion with drooping whiskers.

"You don't look so frightening now," said Mouse bravely. "I think you have a bad attack of soricus throaticus. It's brought on by too much roaring and sleeping in the rain. We can cure you, but if we make you better you must promise not to frighten us again."

Lion tried to say, "I promise," but he could only squeak and nod his head.

132

For two whole days they nursed and comforted Lion; and for two whole nights he slept and dreamed and sneezed and coughed. By the third morning he began to feel better.

The proud and fearless lion stood up and stretched his legs. "Good morning, animals," he said politely. But there was no reply. He walked down his hill and into the jungle calling, "Tiger! Hippo! Giraffe! Little Mouse! Is anybody there?"

But the jungle was as sad and silent as if the animals had never existed.

Lion searched through the jungle for many miles. All of a sudden, the little mouse came scurrying towards him.

"Oh, brave Lion," she cried. "Come quickly. While you were sleeping two hunters came and drove the animals into a cage. They are being taken away from the jungle to join a circus. Because I am so small, I managed to escape through the bars."

135

When Lion heard Mouse's story he began to feel his pride and fearlessness coming back. The jungle would not be the jungle without the animals. "Climb on to my head, little one," he said. "We must go and find them."

On and on they went until they came to the very edge of the jungle. In the moonlight Lion and Mouse could see two hunters sitting by a camp fire. The poor animals were locked in a cage. Elephant's trunk was all squashed up and Giraffe's neck was stuck between the bars.

That night Lion and Mouse lay down together and fell asleep trying to think of a plan to save the animals.

By the time the sun had risen over the jungle the next morning, they had a plan. Mouse sat on top of Lion's head so that only she could be seen over the top of the bush. She squeaked as loudly as she could until the hunters heard her.

"That's the mouse who escaped!" shouted one hunter.

"After her!" called the other.

Lion leaped out from behind the bush, roaring the loudest and most terrifying roar he had ever roared. ROARRRRRRR! "That'll show 'em!" said the proud and fearless lion.

136

137

The terrified hunters fell over, dropping their guns and the keys to the cage. Mouse picked up the keys and ran to free the animals.

As they trooped back home, Lion realised he had never felt quite so proud and fearless before. And he kept his promise never to frighten the animals again.

But if those hunters ever came back . . . well, that would be another story!

139

ROBERT'S WINTER COAT   Michael Glover

It was the hottest day of the year in Smoky Hills National Park, and Robert just didn't know what to do with himself. So he went up to his Momma and asked *her* what he should do.

"Momma," he said, "I'm so hot I could just explode. I wish I didn't have to wear such a big, furry coat as this, either . . ."

Momma just looked at him. He could be so stupid sometimes.

"Go and lie down in the shade of those big rocks beside Pa. You don't have to jump around all the time."

But Robert didn't like that idea at all. He couldn't stand still for more than five seconds together.

"I don't want to, Momma. Anyway, Pa's a fat old lazy thing the way he lies around all day . . ."

140

Grandpa Smokeye, who was sitting close by, nodded his old head and said:

"Let the guy do just as he please, Rosanna . . ."

But Momma took a swipe at him with her paw all the same for being so cheeky.

"Now just you take yourself off some place and stop bothering me, child."

So Robert padded off into the trees. What *could* he do to cool himself?

Then he remembered the animals that lived on the plain, so he followed the stream down the mountain – it was so lovely and cooling to swim through the water! – and when he saw that little huddle of log cabins in the distance, he slipped out of the water and crept along on all fours. He didn't want to frighten them off or anything . . .

When he got up close to the first cabin, he stood up and peered in through the window. The baby ones were sitting round the table, and in the far corner was the Pa, the one he so much wanted to see . . .

He was facing the wall, pawing at his face, just like Robert had seen him do before. Pa turned this way and that, pulling his face about . . . and then it happened. He picked up something long and thin and shiny in his paw, dipped it into a little white bowl, shook it about, and started stroking his face.

Robert wanted to jump for joy when he saw the fur on his face falling away, but he didn't dare. He didn't want to make a noise and spoil everything. So he just stood there, and soon that Pa's face was as smooth and furless as a stone in the desert . . .

Robert crouched down and waited and by and by he heard them opening the door and stamping around outside. And then there was the sound of a gun firing off – that made him wince – followed by a low growl that got louder then fainter and fainter. He peered round the corner of the cabin, and now all he could see was dust settling . . .

Robert was only a small bear, but it didn't take him long to break down the door with his shoulder, scurry inside, pick up the shiny thing, and scamper off home. And running wasn't so hard now anyway because the sun was already going down behind his mountain . . .

Just before dawn, Robert slipped out of the cave where all the rest of the bears were still sleeping, and found himself a quiet, shady spot in the forest. He sat down and stared at the thin, shiny thing in his paw. Then he started to stroke himself on the arm, quite gently at first because he was a little afraid of it, but soon he was making long, sweeping strokes, and at every stroke another bunch of fur fell at his feet!

And a few minutes later he looked so different that he didn't know if his own Ma would even recognise him any more. He wasn't brown and furry any more but smooth and pink all over! Except his toe nails, of course . . .

And when he stood up, he felt so cool and light on his feet that he couldn't stop himself leaping up into the air, and then he did twenty or thirty rolls – backwards, forwards, sideways. He noticed that the dust he'd been rolling in had changed his colour all over again, and now he was the same colour as the earth itself . . .

But he thought he preferred to be a pink bear best of all, so he set about cleaning himself with his tongue, and when he'd finished he felt so tired out that he lay down in the sun and fell asleep.

When Robert woke up again the sun was high in the sky, and when he saw it there, he thought he was going to feel tired and hot all over again, so he started crawling along on all fours ever so slowly, crawling back home. But when he felt the cool breeze blowing across his skin, he looked down at himself and suddenly remembered that he was different now. He was so cool and light that he could run and jump just as he pleased, so he started racing home as fast as his legs would go. He was so eager to show them what he'd done – and so pleased to be the only pink bear in the world!

Momma was lying beside Pa in the shade of that rock with her eyes closed.

"Momma!" he shouted, "look at me, Momma! I'm not hot any more!"

"Don't bother me now, Robert," she said. "I'm sleeping."

"But Momma, look at me! See what I've done to myself . . ."

His Momma sighed and slowly opened one sleepy eye.

"What in heaven's name, Robert," she said, scrabbling up from the ground, "have you gone and done to that beautiful coat of yours?"

"I took it off, Momma. It was so hot . . ."

But he didn't tell her *how* he took it off. He wanted that to be a secret. He didn't want all the other bears being pink all over . . .

Then he heard a voice behind him, the voice of his sister

Clementine, and she was saying:

"Hey, just come and look what Robert's done to himself. He's pink all over – except for the little stripe up his back . . ."

And now they were all standing round him, pointing and laughing, and saying:

"What's that little stripe up your back for, Robert? Are you changing into a skunk or something?"

Robert twisted his head as far as it would go, but he still couldn't see his own back, and he couldn't feel it either, that little strip of fur right down his back, because his arms weren't quite long enough to reach . . .

He hung his head in shame. They were all staring at him now, poking fun at him, and even Pa was frowning down, not saying a single word . . . Only Grandpa Smokeye took his side when he said:

"Let the guy do as he please . . ."

But he was old and nobody listened to him any more, not even Robert.

So Robert crawled back into the forest and sat down under a tree until the sun went down, and then he began to feel cool all over, so cool that he started to shiver in the darkness, and he had to cover his body all over with leaves just to keep warm. And he didn't go back home at all that night, and none of them came looking for him either.

And the next day was the very worst day of Robert's life. The sky changed its colour from blue to grey. And soon a cold wind started blowing and moaning through the trees of the forest, sweeping up the leaves into wet, sticky heaps, and the rains came on, turning the ground to yellow mud.

Robert didn't know where to go to keep warm. He just kept on running until he came to a cave a bit like the one his Ma and Pa lived in and sat in the entrance, staring out, not wet any more but still cold and very miserable. Then he thought to himself: I *need* that coat of mine. If I don't get it back, I'll *freeze* to death . . .

And then he had an idea, another one. He remembered something else about those animals down on the plain . . . So he ran and ran down the mountain side through the driving rain, following the path of that stream again, but this time he didn't jump in and swim because he was already as wet as wet could be, and the stream was high and raging now. And when Robert reached that log cabin, he peeped into the window again.

The first creatures had gone, the ones he'd looked at last time, and now there were just two of them, a Ma and a Pa, and they were both crouched down on the ground, staring into a blazing wall of orange flames, and Robert felt frightened to see that fire because it was fire that ate up the forests and drove them high into the mountains, all of them, not just bears but all the racoons and skunks and everybody else too. Suddenly the Ma stood up, walked over to a big box and lifted something out with her paw. Robert's eyes opened wide. It was a coat, a big brown coat, just like his own . . .

And Robert felt so wild with excitement when he saw it that he ran round to the door of the cabin and started pawing at it, and a second later the Ma opened up, but before he could even tell her what he wanted, she screamed so loud that Robert ran off again, but not very far, just into the shade of some trees nearby. He watched them run out of the door and down the road hand in hand, and the Ma was still screaming and screaming . . .

Robert tore into the cabin, snatched up that coat between his teeth, and ran back to the mountains. And when he got home, still dragging that coat along between his teeth, his Ma said how bad he had been to run off like that, pink bear or no, and how pleased she was to see him again for all his bad ways. But Robert felt so cold and tired that he just pulled his coat into the cave, lay down beside his Pa, and dragged the coat on top of him with his teeth.

And every cold day he did the same, pulling it over him when he lay down to sleep or getting his Ma to lay it across his back when he wanted to walk about in the daytime, but he had to walk very slowly and not shake himself about or the coat would fall off. And if *that* happened, he had to crawl right underneath it again and lift himself up ever so gently . . . Robert didn't do much running and jumping that winter.

But one day he didn't feel so cold any more – even without his coat – and when he told his Ma she looked at him and said:

"That's because you're growing a new coat of your own, Robert."

And when he stared down at himself, he saw that he wasn't really pink any more either. He was turning brown again. And when he touched his skin, he didn't feel smooth any more but a tiny bit bristly . . .

So one morning early in the spring, Robert carried that old coat, his winter coat, back down the mountain between his teeth. He even swam with it in the stream a little way. And he dropped it just outside the door of the cabin, not knowing what else to do because when he peeped in the window the place was empty.

Perhaps those creatures don't live in these parts anymore, he thought to himself.

But he couldn't take that long, thin, shiny thing back as well because it had rusted away in the winter rains . . .

HENNY-PENNY Traditional

One morning Henny-Penny
was pecking corn in
the garden when
– BANG! an acorn fell
down from the sky and
hit her right on the head.

"Goodness gracious me!"
said Henny-Penny. "The sky's
going to fall, I had better go and
tell the King."

So off went Henny-Penny and after
a while she met Cocky-Locky.

"Good-day, Cocky-Locky," she said.

"And a good-day to you, Henny-Penny," said Cocky-Locky.
"And where may you be going so early in the morning?"

"I'm off to tell the King that the sky is falling," said
Henny-Penny.

152

"May I come with you?" said Cocky-Locky.

"Of course you may," said Henny-Penny.

So Henny-Penny and Cocky-Locky went along together to tell the King the sky was falling. They went on and on and on until after a while they met Ducky-Daddles.

"And where may you two be going, Henny-Penny and Cocky-Locky?" asked Ducky-Daddles.

"We're off to tell the King the sky is falling," said Henny-Penny and Cocky-Locky.

"May I come with you?" said Ducky-Daddles.

"Of course you may," said Henny-Penny and Cocky-Locky.

So Henny-Penny and Cocky-Locky and Ducky-Daddles went along together to tell the King the sky was falling. They went on and on and on until after a while they met Goosey-Poosey.

"And where may you be going to, Henny-Penny, Cocky-Locky and Ducky-Daddles?" asked Goosey-Poosey.

"We're off to tell the King the sky is falling," said Henny-Penny, Cocky-Locky and Ducky-Daddles.

"May I come with you?" asked Goosey-Poosey.

"Of course you may," said Henny-Penny, Cocky-Locky and Ducky-Daddles.

So Henny-Penny, Cocky-Locky, Ducky-Daddles and Goosey-Poosey went off together to tell the King the sky was falling. They walked on and on and on until after a while they met Turkey-Lurkey.

"And where may you be going to, Henny-Penny, Cocky-Locky, Ducky-Daddles and Goosey-Poosey?" asked Turkey-Lurkey.

"We're going to tell the King the sky's falling," said Henny-Penny, Cocky-Locky, Ducky-Daddles and Goosey-Poosey.

"May I come with you?" asked Turkey-Lurkey.

"Of course you may," said Henny-Penny, Cocky-Locky, Ducky-Daddles and Goosey-Poosey.

So Henny-Penny, Cocky-Locky, Ducky-Daddles,
Goosey-Poosey and Turkey-Lurkey all went off together to tell
the King the sky was falling. And they walked on and on until
after a while they met Foxy-Woxy.

"And where may all of you be going to this fine morning,
Henny-Penny, Cocky-Locky, Ducky-Daddles, Goosey-Poosey
and Turkey-Lurkey?" asked Foxy-Woxy.

156

"If you really must know," said Henny-Penny,
Cocky-Locky, Ducky-Daddles, Goosey-Poosey and
Turkey-Lurkey, "we're all off to tell the King that the sky
is falling."

"But oh," said Foxy-Woxy, "but oh, this isn't the way to
where the King lives, Henny-Penny, Cocky-Locky,
Ducky-Daddles, Goosey-Poosey and Turkey-Lurkey. If you
follow me, I'll show you the right way. Would you all like to
come with me?"

"Oh, that is indeed very kind of you, Foxy-Woxy," said
Henny-Penny, Cocky-Locky, Ducky-Daddles, Goosey-Poosey
and Turkey-Lurkey.

So Henny-Penny, Cocky-Locky, Ducky-Daddles,
Goosey-Poosey, Turkey-Lurkey and Foxy-Woxy all went along
together to tell the King that the sky was falling.
And they went on and on and on
until after a while they came
to a dark, dark hole.

Now this dark, dark hole was really the door of Foxy-Woxy's den. But of course, Foxy-Woxy was too foxy to let them know this. Instead he said: "This is a short cut to where the King lives. If you follow me we'll get there in next to no time. Let me go first and you come after me, Henny-Penny, Cocky-Locky, Ducky-Daddles, Goosey-Poosey and Turkey-Lurkey."

158

"Why, of course we'll follow you, of course, of course," replied Henny-Penny, Cocky-Locky, Ducky-Daddles, Goosey-Poosey and Turkey-Lurkey.

So Foxy-Woxy went into his dark, dark den but he didn't go very far inside the dark, dark den. Instead he turned round and waited for Henny-Penny, Cocky-Locky, Ducky-Daddles, Goosey-Poosey and Turkey-Lurkey to follow in after him.

What Foxy-Woxy meant to do when they were all inside was to eat them all up. But luckily for Henny-Penny, Cocky-Locky, Ducky-Daddles, Goosey-Poosey and Turkey-Lurkey, just as they were about to go into the dark cave, a little bird, perched on the branch of a tree, saw them all and guessed what was going to happen. So he called out very loudly:

"Be careful, Henny-Penny, Cocky-Locky, Ducky-Daddles, Goosey-Poosey and Turkey-Lurkey. If you don't want Foxy-Woxy to eat you all up, you'd better turn back and run home as fast as you can."

And only just in time they all turned back and ran home as fast as ever they could. So old Foxy-Woxy didn't have his nice dinner after all. And the King never knew that they thought the sky was going to fall.

MILLIONS OF CATS   Wanda Ga'g

Once upon a time there was a very old man and a very old woman. They lived in a nice clean house which had flowers all around it, except where the door was. But they couldn't be happy because they were so very lonely.

"If we only had a cat!" sighed the very old woman.
"A cat?" asked the very old man.
"Yes, a sweet little fluffy cat," said the very old woman.
"I will get you a cat, my dear," said the very old man.

And he set out over the hills to look for one. He climbed over the sunny hills. He trudged through the cool valleys. He walked a long, long time and at last he came to a hill which was quite covered with cats.

Cats here, cats there,
Cats and kittens everywhere,
Hundreds of cats,
Thousands of cats,
Millions and billions and trillions of cats.

"Oh!" cried the old man joyfully. "Now I can choose the prettiest cat and take it home with me!" So he chose one. It was white.

But just as he was about to leave, he saw another one all black and white and it seemed just as pretty as the first. So he took this one also.

But then he saw a fuzzy grey kitten way over here which was every bit as pretty as the others so he took it too.

And now he saw one way down in a corner which he thought too lovely to leave so he took this too.

And just then, over here, the very old man found a kitten which was black and very beautiful.

"It would be a shame to leave that one," said the very old man. So he took it.

And now, over there, he saw a cat which had brown and yellow stripes like a baby tiger.

"I simply must take it!" cried the very old man, and he did.

So it happened that every time the very old man looked up, he saw another cat which was so pretty he could not bear to leave it, and before he knew it, he had chosen them all.

And so he went back over the sunny hills and down through the cool valleys, to show all his pretty kittens to the very old woman.

It was very funny to see those hundreds and thousands and millions and billions and trillions of cats following him.

They came to a pond.

"Mew, mew! We are thirsty!" cried the

Hundreds of cats,

Thousands of cats,

Millions and billions and trillions of cats.

"Well, here is a great deal of water," said the very old man.
Each cat took a sip of water, and the pond was gone!
"Mew, mew! Now we are hungry!" said the
Hundreds of cats,
Thousands of cats,
Millions and billions and trillions of cats.

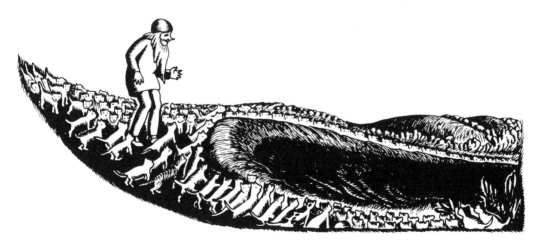

"There is much grass on the hills," said the very old man.
Each cat ate a mouthful of grass and not a blade was left!
Pretty soon the very old woman saw them coming.

"My dear!" she cried. "What are you doing? I asked for one little cat, and what do I see? –

Cats here, cats there,
Cats and kittens everywhere,
Hundreds of cats,
Thousands of cats,
Millions and billions and trillions of cats.

"But we can never feed them all," said the very old woman. "They will eat us out of house and home."

"I never thought of that," said the very old man. "What shall we do?"

The very old woman thought for a while and then she said, "I know! We will let the cats decide which one we should keep."

"Oh yes," said the very old man, and he called to the cats, "Which one of you is the prettiest?"

"I am!"

"I am!"

"No, I am!"

"No, I am the prettiest!" "I am!"

"No, I am! I am! I am!" cried hundreds and thousands and millions and billions and trillions of voices, for each cat thought itself the prettiest.

And they began to quarrel.

They bit and scratched and clawed each other and made such a great noise that the very old man and the very old woman ran into the house as fast as they could. They did not like such quarrelling. But after a while the noise stopped and the very old man and the very old woman peeped out of the window to see what had happened. They could not see a single cat!

"I think they must have eaten each other all up," said the very old woman. "It's too bad!"

"But look!" said the very old man, and he pointed to a bunch of high grass. In it sat one little frightened kitten. They went out and picked it up. It was thin and scraggly.

"Poor little kitty," said the very old woman.

"Dear little kitty," said the very old man, "how does it happen that you were not eaten up with all those hundreds and thousands and millions and billions and trillions of cats?"

"Oh, I'm just a very homely little cat," said the kitten, "so when you asked who was the prettiest I didn't say anything. So nobody bothered about me."

They took the kitten into the house, where the very old woman gave it a warm bath and brushed its fur until it was soft and shiny.

Every day they gave it plenty of milk – and soon it grew nice and plump.

"And it is a very pretty cat, after all!" said the very old woman.

"It is the most beautiful cat in the whole world," said the very old man. "I ought to know, for I've seen –

Hundreds of cats,

Thousands of cats,

Millions and billions and trillions of cats –

and not one is as pretty as this one."

ACKNOWLEDGMENTS

All possible care has been taken to make full acknowledgment in every case where material is still in copyright. If errors have occurred, they will be corrected in subsequent editions if notification is sent to the publisher. Grateful acknowledgment is made for permission to reprint the following:

'Elephant Big and Elephant Little' and 'Pig says Positive' from *The Anita Hewett Animal Story Book* by Anita Hewett (The Bodley Head). Reproduced by permission of the author.
'The Lion and his Friends' © 1991 by Anne Forsyth. Reproduced by permission of the author.
'The Ossopit Tree' and 'Monkeying About' by Stephen Corrin. Reproduced by permission of the author.
'How the Polar Bear Became' by Ted Hughes. Reprinted by permission of Faber and Faber Ltd from *How the Whale Became and Other Stories* by Ted Hughes.
'The Shooting' from *Fantastic Mr Fox* by Roald Dahl (Unwin Hyman and Penguin Books Ltd)
'Dragons and Giants' from *Frog and Toad Together* by Arnold Lobel (Worlds Work Limited, 1973)
'The Friendliest Dog in the World' © 1991 by Anne Forsyth. Reproduced by permission of the author.
'Tim Rabbit's Party' by Alison Uttley. Reprinted by permission of Faber and Faber Ltd from *The Adventures of Tim Rabbit* by Alison Uttley.
'The Proud and Fearless Lion' by Ann and Reg Cartwright. Reproduced by permission of Hutchinson Children's Books.
'Robert's Winter Coat' © 1991 by Michael Glover. Reproduced by permission of the author.
'Millions of Cats' by Wanda Ga'g. Reprinted by permission of Faber and Faber Ltd from *Millions of Cats* by Wanda Ga'g.

ILLUSTRATION ACKNOWLEDGMENTS

The Publisher wishes to thank the following:

'The Lion and his Friends'. Illustrations by Karin Van Heerden. Reproduced by permission of the artist.
'The Three Little Pigs'. Illustrations by L. Leslie Brooke.
'The Hare and the Tortoise'. Illustrations © 1991 by Michael O'Mara Books Ltd.
'Dragons and Giants'. Illustrations by Arnold Lobel. Reproduced from *Frog and Toad Together* by Arnold Lobel (Worlds Work Limited, 1973).
'The Proud and Fearless Lion'. Illustrations by Ann and Reg Cartwright. Reproduced by permission of Hutchinson Children's Books.
'Millions of Cats'. Illustrations by Wanda Ga'g. Reprinted by permission of Faber and Faber Ltd from *Millions of Cats* by Wanda Ga'g.
All other illustrations © 1991 by Martin Ursell.

176